# ABC My Hair and Me

*Learning About My Hair with Help from the ABCs*

Written By: Miyosha Streets

Illustrated By: Sarah Gamal

Written   by   Miyosha   Streets
Illustrated by Sarah Gamal

ISBN: 978-0-578-56076-2
Library of Congress Control Number:2019911844

Printed in the United States.
Post Office Box 2223
Lancaster, South Carolina 29721

Published October 2019.

*From London to Liberty*
*And everyone in-between*

*May you forever be represented*
*And always seen*

**A** is for **Afro**.
**Wear it with pride.**

# B

**B** is for **Braids**.
With parts on the side.

# C

**C** is for **Curls.**

## The more the merrier.

**D** is for **Dreadlocs**.
For boys and for girls.

**E**

**E is for Eye-catching.**
**Your hair is the view.**

**F**

**F** is for **Frizzy**.
Wear your hair free.

# G

**G is for Gorgeous.**
**That is what you are to me.**

# H

# H is for Healthy Hair.
## Always take care.

# I

**I** is for **Inches**.

**That will grow with care and patience.**

**J** is for **J**oy.
**Your hair is inspiration.**

**K** is for **Kinky**.
**Your coily hair is beautiful.**

# L

**L** is the **L**ove
**You have for your hair.**

**M is for Moisture.**
**Dry hair beware.**

**N** is for **Natural**.
**All hair is good hair.**

# O is for Oil.
## Essential food for your hair.

# P

**P** is for **Puffs.**

You should wear a pair.

# Q

**Q** is for **Queen.**
**The crown is your hair.**

**R** is for **Rods.**

**Roll your hair to make fun curls.**

# S

**S is for Shrinkage.**
**Your hair is magic.**

# T

**T is for Twist.**
**Extra textures we love.**

# U

**U is for Unique.**
**For that you should be proud of.**

# V

**V is for Versatile.**

**Oh, my! All the styles you can wear.**

# W

**W** is the **Water**
**You give daily to your hair.**

# X is for the eXtraordinary child that you are.

**Y** is the **Y**ummy
**Smells that come from your hair.**

# Z

**Z is for the Zig Zag styles that you wear.**

# No matter the color, length, texture, or styling.

Your HAIR is BEAUTIFUL so keep on SMILING.

CPSIA information can be obtained
at www.ICGtesting.com
Printed in the USA
LVHW071518181121
703738LV00007B/490